Happy

Tim and Tig

Victor Kelleher

Illustrated by Judy Watson

HAPPY CAT BOOKS

For Scott with my love. *J. W.*

Published by
Happy Cat Books
An imprint of Catnip Publishing Ltd
14 Greville Street
London EC1N 8SB

First published by Penguin Books, Australia, 2007

This edition first published 2011
3 5 7 9 10 8 6 4 2

Text copyright © Victor Kelleher, 2007
Illustrations copyright © Judy Watson, 2007

A CIP catalogue record for this book is available from the
British Library

ISBN 978-1-905117-81-9

Printed in India

www.catnippublishing.co.uk

CHAPTER
ONE

Tim was given lots of presents for his birthday. The best one of all came from Aunt Ethel.

'Here,' she said, and she handed Tim a **very large** kitten.

He loved it. So did Mum

and Dad. They loved its
orange and black stripes,
and its big floppy paws.

'A word of advice,' said
Aunt Ethel, who was bossy.

'Never feed it any meat.
Dry cat food is best.'

'Nonsense,' said Dad. 'A
growing kitten needs meat.'

Aunt Ethel didn't like

being contradicted. 'Don't
say you weren't warned!'
she said, and she walked
off in a huff.

Nobody noticed. They
were too interested in
the kitten.

'I'll call him Tig,'
Tim said.

'G-G-G-R-O-W-L,' Tig
said, biting a hole in the
tablecloth.

'The poor dear,' Mum

said. 'He must be hungry.'

Tig bit a hole in the

armchair.

'Famished, by the looks of him,' Dad said.

'Got anything for his tea?' Tim asked.

'I have just the thing,' Mum said.

She went to the fridge and took out a dish of **raw meat**.

CHAPTER TWO

'Look at him,' Mum said.

'Isn't he a darling?'

'He's the best,' Tim said.

Tig lay asleep on the rug.
He had grown in the past
month. He was bigger than
most dogs.

'He's having a dream,'
said Dad.

Tig twitched . . . and
twitched again. One paw
shot out and tore the end
off the rug.

'There, there,' Tim said,
patting Tig's head.

Mum sat down on a milk
crate – mainly because

there was nowhere else to
sit. The lounge suite looked
like something savaged by
a chainsaw.

Tig slept on. Another twitch, and he tore the leg off a chair.

'A bad dream, by the looks of it,' Dad said.

'That last side of lamb probably disagreed with him,' Mum said.

'What about steak?' Tim suggested. 'That may settle his stomach.'

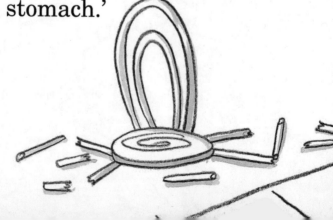

Mum went to the fridge.
As the door clicked open, so
did Tig's eyes.

He licked hungrily at his
enormous fangs.

'R-R-R-O-A-R-R!'
said Tig.

'That's my cat,' Tim
said proudly.

'Here, kitty-kitty,' Mum
called.

CHAPTER
THREE

Three months passed. Tig was now the size of a pony. The house had changed too. It looked like the local tip.

At that moment Tig was trying to bite off a door handle.

'I reckon he's bored,'
Mum said.

'Couldn't agree more,'
Dad said. 'A growing cat
needs exercise.'

'Tell you what,' Tim said.
'I'll take him to the shops.'
Tim attached a skinny
lead to Tig's collar and
marched off down the street.

'Look after him,' Mum called. 'Remember, he's only a kitten.'

The shopping centre was crowded when Tim arrived, but pretty soon there was hardly a person to be seen. People lay hidden behind clothes racks and litter bins. Others had scampered into shops.

Tig liked this hide-and-seek game. He leaped at

a man who was pretending
to be a statue.

'He only wants to play,'
Tim said.

The man also wanted

to play. He dived into
the fountain.

Next, Tig spotted
a woman under a bench.
He scooped her out and

gave her a few friendly
pats. Tim could see she
wasn't bothered, from the
way she closed her eyes
and went to sleep.

Quite a few people
seemed sleepy. The minute
Tig grabbed them, they
drifted off. Tim wondered
whether they'd had too
much lunch.

Thoughts of lunch made
Tim notice a butcher's shop.

He went to buy Tig some
meat.

The butcher was very
kind. He wouldn't accept
money. 'Have anything

you want!' he said, and
he locked himself in the
cool-room.

Tim let Tig decide, as
a reward for being so good.

Tig chose a turkey and ate
it in two bites.

The shopping centre still
looked empty when they
left.

Funny, that, thought Tim.
Friday must be a slack day.

CHAPTER FOUR

Another three months passed. Tig now had a lair in the attic.

'It's not good for him, up there on his own,' Mum said.

'You're right,' Dad agreed. 'He needs to mix with his own kind.'

'What if I take him to the
cat show in the park?' Tim
said.

He attached the same
skinny lead to Tig's collar
and led him off.

There were hundreds of

cats in the park. Tig was excited. He bounded over to them.

'Y-E-O-O-W-W!' screeched the cats.

'E-E-E-E-E!' screamed their owners.

They all began climbing trees.

That's odd, thought Tim. The papers said this was a cat show, not a tree-climbing contest.

He looked around. The
only people still at ground
level were the judges. Tim
guessed they must be cold,

because they were shaking
all over. To his amazement,
they shoved a big silver cup
towards him.

Printed on the cup were the words CHAMPION CAT.

Tim felt very proud. 'Hey, Tig,' he called. 'See what you've won.'

Tig let out a roar, to show how happy he was.

The judges also climbed a tree then.

I wish they'd make up their minds, thought Tim. Is this a cat show or what?

He nearly let them see

how well Tig could climb.

But when he took Tig

over to the nearest tree,
everyone bailed out. People
and cats leaped around like
monkeys.

Tim decided they were
silly, and he led Tig home.

CHAPTER FIVE

Tim's class at school was having a Pets Day.

Tim and Tig arrived late – because every time they crossed a street, cars swerved into each other. Tim couldn't understand it. He tried telling his teacher,

but she took one look at Tig
and dozed off.

The kids weren't at all
sleepy. They scrambled up

bookshelves and crowded
onto the tall cupboard in the
corner. Most of their pets
dived through the window.

It was mainly the dogs
that stayed. They stood
there making smelly
puddles. So did some of
the kids.

'R-R-R-O-O-O-A-A-A-R-R-R!' said Tig.

The kids and their dogs
wet themselves more. A few
fell off the cupboard.

Then the teacher woke
up and started singing.
At least, it sounded like

singing. It was a kind of
E-E-E-E-E sound.

Tig was fond of music,
so he had a go too.

'G-R-O-W-O-O-O-L!'

The fire alarm joined in.

'DING-A-LING-A-LING!'

The rest of the school

added a drumbeat by
stampeding along the
corridor.

Tim decided it was
a pretty neat sound. Better
than those symphony
concerts Dad listened to.

Tig wasn't quite so
pleased. But he perked up
when the school principal
appeared. It turned out
that she liked playing tag.

Tig chased her round
and round the school. She
spoiled the game in the end
by climbing a tree.

What's with all this tree-climbing? Tim wondered.

He and Tig had a good walk home. It was fun watching people swing from street lights and dive into prickly hedges. Some could run even faster than the school principal.

Tim didn't take much notice of the car crashes. He'd got used to those.

CHAPTER
SIX

Tim was woken next
morning by lots of noise
in the street.

'This neighbourhood
isn't what it used to be,'
Dad said.

They looked out of
the window. There were

police and firefighters and
soldiers everywhere. Plus
fire engines and tanks and
armoured cars.

'It must be those war

games you hear about,'
Mum said.

'Yeah, but why in our
front garden?' Dad said.

As he spoke, a tank

flattened the hedge. A
fire engine squashed the
flowerbed. Armoured cars
smashed the side fence.

'The mayor will hear
about this,' Dad said.

The mayor had heard
already. He came waddling
up the front path. A general,
the fire officer and the police
chief came too.

The family went to meet
them at the front door.

'We have reason to
believe you're harbouring
a dangerous animal,' the
mayor said.

Mum looked puzzled.
'Dangerous animal?'

The general puffed up his
chest. 'We are speaking of
your wild creature.'

'Wild creature?' Dad said,
and scratched his head.

The fire officer nodded.
'We refer, sir, to your
tropical feline.'

'Tropical feline?' Tim said.

'Don't play dumb with
us,' the police chief said.

'We know about your exotic beast.'

'Exotic beast?' Tim, Mum and Dad said together.

Tig chose that moment

to come down from his lair.

'G-G-G-R-R-R-R!'

he said.

The visitors suddenly
looked ill. They clutched
at each other and went
a horrible colour.

'Th-that's the a-animal
in qu-question,' said
the mayor.

Mum could hardly believe
her ears. 'You can't mean
our darling Tig!'

Tim tickled Tig under
the chin. 'Yeah, he's just
a pussy cat.'

'No way!' the visitors
answered. 'That's a **tiger**!'

'You're kidding us!' Mum
and Dad said.

They took a good look

at Tig all the same. So did Tim. For the first time, they noticed how long his claws were. How huge his fangs. How big his muscles. How wild his whiskers.

Tig helped by yawning.
Quite a lot happened then.
The general and the fire
officer fell asleep, and the
mayor leaped into the
police chief's arms.

'What else can he be but a tiger?' the mayor squeaked.

Dad stroked his chin thoughtfully. 'Yeah, maybe you've got a point there.'

CHAPTER
SEVEN

The mayor ordered Tig to be taken to the zoo.

A lion tamer arrived at the house that afternoon. He flicked his whip and tried to shoo Tig into an armoured van.

Tig had never seen

a whip before. He ate it in
one bite.

The tamer brought out a
poky stick.

Tig loved sticks. He
crunched this one in two.
The tamer mopped his
brow. 'I'll try him with

my dart gun,' he said.

Tig had never seen an air rifle either. He bent it in half.

'He's too savage for me,' the tamer said. 'We'll have to shoot him.'

Mum got really angry. 'No one's shooting our pussy cat!'

'How else can we move him?' asked the tamer.

'I'll show you,' Tim said.

He clicked the skinny lead onto Tig's collar and led him away.

The zoo manager seemed to be expecting them. He was perched on a tall shelf in his office. 'It's cooler up here,' he said.

Tim didn't find it hot. But Mum had taught him never to contradict grown-ups. 'Where should I put Tig?' he asked.

'There's an empty cage down among the big cats.' Tim forgot what Mum had said about not

contradicting grown-ups.

'You're not putting Tig in a

cage!' he yelled.

'Be reasonable,' said the

zoo manager. 'He's a fierce
and dangerous animal.
No one can change that,
can they?'

Tim had a think.
'Maybe they can,' he
said at last. 'Mind if
I use your phone?'

Tim's call lasted a while – though mostly he just listened and said things like 'I'm sorry, Aunt Ethel' and 'No, I won't forget this time.'

He looked quite relieved when he rang off. 'Here's the plan . . .' he told the zoo manager.

CHAPTER
EIGHT

Tig became famous. There were headlines about him in the papers.

TIG THE NOT-SO-TERRIBLE, said one.

TIG THE TENDER, said another.

'This tiger gives new hope

to a violent world,' said
the mayor.

People flocked to the zoo.
They wanted to see a tiger
who was gentle and didn't
need to live in a cage.

Reporters photographed
him playing with kids.
'Why is he so peace-loving?'
they asked. 'How come he
doesn't eat people?'

Mum and Dad beamed
with pride. 'He was well
brought up,' they explained.
'Just like our Tim.'

A reporter pointed to

where Tig was licking
a woman's hand. 'Yeah,
but he could have a mid-
morning snack right now if
he wanted. What's stopping
him?'

Tim answered for the whole family, Aunt Ethel included. 'It's simple really. We always make sure he has a good breakfast.'

The reporter wasn't convinced. 'A good breakfast? That can't be all.'

'Oh, there is one other small thing,' Tim admitted with a grin. 'We **never, ever, ever** feed him meat.'

FROM VICTOR KELLEHER

Have you noticed how most people think their pets
are the best ever? People with growly dogs think
they're gentle; people with scratchy cats think they're
friendly. So how would it be if someone had a pet
python? Or a pet gorilla! Or better still, a pet TIGER!
It was this last idea that got me started on *Tim &
Tig*. And because I love tigers nearly as much as I
love gorillas, I had to give the story a happy ending.
But what would happen if someone *really* had a tiger
for a pet . . .?
No, maybe it's better not to think too much
about that! After all, dear old Tig wouldn't hurt a
fly . . . would he????
Here, kitty-kitty.

FROM JUDY WATSON

My dad is a vet, and when I was a little girl our
house was at the back of his vet clinic. I got used to
having lots of animals around and hearing animal
noises all night long. Sometimes I climbed into the
big cages to pat the animals who were in hospital
feeling rotten.
I was a bit like Tim, because I didn't seem to notice
that some of the animals were *very* big and had *very*
large teeth. Some of them had sore heads or tummy
aches or broken bones. I bet they wished
I would leave them alone!
I think I was very lucky not to have been chewed to
bits.